A Battleaxe and a Metal Arm 9:

Ghost in the Wheelhouse

Samuel Fleming

Cover Art by David Leahey

ISBN-13: 978-1-954679-23-8 (paperback)
ISBN-13: 978-1-954679-22-1 (ebook)

Thank you to my Beta Readers

and to my First Reader,

Mel.

Contents

"Many have tried to reconcile
their place in this world. Some
occasionally find peace. For a
time."
—undefined

Previously...

After waking, Helesys and Taunauk mused about how they would've met—a banished Endroggen, an elven weaver, and a rogue. Perhaps they had all been outcasts. Their only guesses were that their motley group had been chasing someone or had been chased by someone.

They came to a massive cavern covered by glowing flowers, a structure that stretched so far and so high that they could not see the end of it through the mist.

The heroes followed the cavern until they came to an ornate stone wall, a barrier that completely sealed off an ancient city. There they encountered a group of creatures marked by black 'X''s on their faces—the mark of the parasite and one of the lingering deaths of the dungeon. There was no reasoning with the infected, and Helesys and Taunauk were forced to cut them down.

Using her wand-arm, Helesys translated the ancient writings and spoke the words to open the stone doors and continue forward—the ancient word for dreams. Inside, they found dozens more infected, and the heroes used the close confines of the hallway to funnel and destroy them. When all was still, they found more writing and a stash of magic totems, tended by the same small, silent faeries from the flooded temple of the fishmen. If the writings were to be believed, then the city of Shéslang had fallen to the parasite.

Taunauk voiced his reluctance, having twice been at the mercy of lingering deaths. Despite this, Helesys ushered them on. Her wand-arm was leading them deeper into the caverns and into the lost city.

She spoke the words and opened the doors to the City of Shéslang, and found a hellscape inside. The city had become a writhing, covered mass of parasites.

Helesys and Taunauk called upon the jade lemur, the totem Helesys took from the city gate, and took to the sky. High above, they found the familiar glow of the flowers while the city screamed the song of the Duoausongur.

But their journey through the upper reaches of the cavern was not peaceful, either. They were accosted by a group of flying lemur—creatures who took insult to Helesys, Taunauk, and their made-thing jade lemur. The heroes were escorted to the inner caverns of the Missives, elder lemurs who spoke for the warren.

Helesys and Taunauk explained their plight, to reach the end of the cavern, to find the final resting place of the serpent Shéslang. After some deliberation, the Missives allowed the heroes to leave and continue their journey in peace.

They flew on and the cavern seemed to grow smaller before they came to a towering parasite-covered structure that stretched to the limits of the cavern. The song of the parasite grew deafening, and for the first time, Helesys could understand its terrible utterings, nothing but the words, "I HUNGER."

Helesys and Taunauk avoided the arms of the parasite, but were forced to land in another set of caverns, seeking passage around the towering monstrosity outside. But inside the caverns were no safer, for both heroes felt the oppressive touch of a malevolent mind following them. Just when Helesys thought they had found the exit, a second Taunauk appeared in the gloom… beckoning her and confusing her.

It took her rage and countering the creature's magic to reveal the true Taunauk. Sickly blue Terrans with psychic powers were huddled in the caves. Creatures who used to hide among the City of Shéslang, but were growing desperate and mad in their isolation.

Helesys and Taunauk fled through the tunnels and back to the main cavern, again taking to the relative safety of the air on the back of the jade lemur.

The sprawling cavern rose up into the mist, and the heroes followed it. They were met by a downpour of infected creatures—leaping from the walls and falling in a mad attempt to grasp the heroes. They fought and fly upward, then hid in an alcove during the worst of the downpour of parasite. When the song of the Duoausongur fell to silence, they flew upward to the rocky ends.

They walked through the final tunnel as it shrunk until it was barely big enough for them to walk through. They rested in the tunnel, spoke of the voice, and how their memories were used against them by the psychic blue-skinned creatures. In spite of reservations, the pair resolved to trust each other and to trust Shawn.

A snake slithered to them, with flat face and mottled green scales. The meager creature revealed itself to be Shéslang, the god-serpent who created the miles of cavern in its wake. Its kind is born feral and powerful, and as they age they grow both powerful and cognizant. In the end, Shéslang revealed itself to be infected by the parasite of its own volition, choosing to succumb to infection rather than be reborn as a rampaging god.

The serpent offered them knowledge, a boon, and a path: Knowledge of three brothers who once sought the Wolf-King and failed. A boon of a magic spear—the Gar of Shéslang. A path through a seam of the realms—

They were to search for the Cogheart—beings that could help Helesys understand her wand and the magic of the seams. Then they were to seek the realm of ice and the Godpeak—where spirits commune and Taunauk could learn the secrets of his glowing power and the spirits within him.

They stepped through the seam to the realm of the Cogheart with new resolve. And they found Shawn on the other side.

~ ~ ~

Reunion

Helesys and Taunauk embraced their comrade. Though they had been apart for only a single realm, it felt much longer to the barbarian and the weaver.

"Yeah, yeah. It felt much longer to me too," Shawn said, embracing them back.

They spent the next hour regaling Shawn of their journey through the titanic caverns and the hellscape that was the City of Shéslang. They told him of the parasite covered city, the colony of flying lemurs, and the chilling encounter with the psychic blue Terrans. They told him of Shéslang, the spear and the path. Then of the Cogheart and how they could help Helesys. And then of the Godpeak and how the spirits there could help Taunauk.

The rogue shook his head and fumbled in his pocket. "That's a *stercus*-load better than what I got. I got chased through a jungle by a bunch of bloodthirsty lizards, then a *big* blood thirsty lizard. Found a tavern, nearly got eaten by said tavern, then got eaten by the big lizard, and all I got for it was this stinking coin!" Shawn pulled out a gold coin, held it up for emphasis, and stared at it. "*I said*, and all I got for it was this sticking coin!"

Silence.

Helesys and Taunauk shared a concerned glance.

"It's good we've found you again," she said. "Clearly, solo adventuring has taken something out of you."

Shawn sighed and pocketed the coin. "Well, now that you can walk between realms without dying, perhaps we can keep together and I can keep a portion of my sanity."

Taunauk chuckled in a low, deep rumble. "You wish to be sane Terrans in an insane world. No wonder we are ill-equipped for our journey."

Shawn wagged a finger at the barbarian. "Taunauk… Stop making sense."

"What of the Voice on the white beach?" Helesys asked. She described it speaking to both her and Taunauk, its vague direction to find both the giant Zhug and the Machine of Antrikaumora. That defeating the Wolf-King would secure their escape. "Did you speak with it too?"

Shawn nodded stiffly. "Yes. I got much the same information and explanation as you did. Except it called me by a different name—*Soldei Milent..*" He said the name carefully, as if trying it on.

The weaver and barbarian shared a glance.

Helesys said coyly, "Shawn *did* sound like a strange name."

The rogue smirked. "Stranger that both names feel right. As if I've gone by both for considerable time... "He waved a dismissive hand. "That's not important. I asked the Voice why I didn't wake up alongside the both of you, yet our fates seem intertwined. The Voice said that you are elf and human, and that I am neither." He slipped back his hood, revealing his sharp, tan features—the most striking were his ears: The right that was pointed like an elf's and the left that was rounded like a human's. Both natural.

The rogue replied, "Unfortunately, the Voice declined to add *what* that made me."

Taunauk shrugged. "Merely the offspring of mixed parentage."

Helesys eyed his features, from ears to jaw, to his piercing blue eyes and back to his ears. Taunauk's idea was more innocent than hers. She had seen so many made-things in their time wandering the dungeon that she worried Shawn might've been another one. Either way, it was a clue to how he was immune to the siren song that he nearly claimed so many aboard the *Malorienta*.

Not that his origin mattered much to the elf—an ally was an ally. A friend was a friend.

So Helesys asked a different question. "You said both names feel right. What would you like us to call you?"

The rogue smiled in appreciation. "Shawn is fine for now, I think. When we stand before the Wolf-King or if we're dining with fine company, I reserve the right to change my mind."

~

They finished telling Shawn about their reclaimed memories: Of Helesys's mother and her sister. Of Helesys's short hair, cut so she could join the elven legion, and merely under illusion to look long. Taunauk spoke of his questions about the axe—a family heirloom that he should not have kept as an exile. Shawn listened with respectful silence.

For the first time, they walked the long, torchlit hallway together, and the air felt lighter for it. Taunauk led, while Helesys and Shawn followed just behind him.

Shawn whispered, "You move pretty quietly, outlander, but I can't help but think I should be going first. Scouting ahead, that sort of thing."

Taunauk grumbled. "You are *not wrong*, but I am in front for now."

Helesys smiled. *This was how it should be*, she thought. When Shawn was gone, she had felt a lack. With him here so early in the realm, it had only confirmed her feelings.

But conversation slowed as lightning began to flash in the distance, at the limits of the hall. Wind whipped down the corridor.

A mile later, the hallway ended on a rocky hillside made of black and jagged stone. The night sky above flickered with constant lightning and churned with stormwinds so loud they had to shout to be heard. The musky smell of rain lingered in the air.

"Which way?" Shawn called beside them.

Taunauk scanned the horizon, shrugged, and turned to Helesys. "I see nothing. What does your wand tell you?"

Helesys looked out over the blackened hills but focused on her gauntlet. There was faint direction… very faint compared to that which she felt in the caverns of Shéslang. If the latter had been stoic guidance, what she felt then was the meekest whisper. For the first time, it seemed as if her wand did not know which way to go.

The weaver pointed out over the rocky hills, following the faint direction.

"You don't seem certain," Shawn said.

"I'm not," the weaver replied, "but that's all we've got."

Shawn raised an eyebrow. "What are your thoughts on flying?"

Helesys shrugged and pulled the jade lemur statuette from her pocket. She frowned, for she didn't feel anything from it. *"Messoris umbra, matris' vellus, ventus equitem,"* she said, but felt only the faintest answer from the stone.

Old realizations came back, and she explained to her comrades. "Not all magic items are as resilient as others. We used much of its power in the caverns, and it needs longer to replenish."

Shawn's head hung low as he turned out to the immense landscape. "It was worth a shot."

~

The heroes knew no peace as they crossed the hills. Their eyes scanned the blurred horizon where black storm met dark plains, and the hills were jagged rocks that could've belied smaller dangers. They moved cautiously over the uneven terrain. Helesys used the Gar of Shéslang as a walking stick and kindled strength to help with balance. They kept weapons at the ready and walked most of the way in silence, even though they saw no other souls.

At one point, Shawn said over the wind, "This is a wasteland if I ever saw one. Can we go back to the *Malorienta?*"

"No," Helesys and Taunauk replied in unison.

~

They walked a mile over the rocky hills before they came across any sign of another creature.

Taunauk pointed to something in the distance that looked to be a Terran in ragged clothes climbing over the rocks. Every few feet, they turned over the black stones and peered beneath them.

The heroes watched with interest until the Terran caught sight of them. It startled and stood up, but instead of the form of the Terran, its face was ghostly white. Its body was long and slender and appeared to be supported by four hind legs.

The creature held up a solitary finger, as if telling them to wait one moment. Then it went back to searching the rocks and meandering up the hill to the three of them.

At one point in its rummaging, it grasped a smoother, spiral shaped rock and held it up to its face. The white of its face slid back like a mask and it sucked out something bright blue and writhing. The white mask slid back over its face, then it tossed the black shell over its shoulder.

"Now that's a strange fellow," Shawn muttered, so quietly Helesys nearly missed it.

As it crawled toward them, Helesys realized that it was much bigger than it first appeared. Out of the corner of her eye, the rogue tensed with twin daggers tucked close to his chest.

It stopped ten feet away from them and stood up, tall enough to look Taunauk in the eye even though it stood further down the hill. The creature was not a Terran in the sense of an elf or human. It wore a mass of colorful rags that seemed both piled on its shoulders and stitched together, draping over its slender, curving torso. It perched on four hind legs, the hip joints of which were close together. Its pair of arms hung limp at its side. The limbs were all dull twists of silver and steel, like cables rather than joints of armor. Its face was white, smooth, and still—like a porcelain mask. Beady black eyes flit to each of three of them.

"Do you speak?" Helesys called over the winds.

"This one does," it replied in a high, smooth voice, like a sword sliding into a sheath. Face unmoving.

"We seek the Cogheart," Helesys said. She held up her metal arm and pulled back the sleeve. "The serpent Shéslang helped us find this realm. I seek answers about my arm and we seek knowledge of how to walk unbidden between realms."

The creature's eyes glanced several times from her gauntlet to Helesys and back again. Thunder rolled in the distance.

"My name is Porthmeus. I can show you the way."

~

Porthmeus led them another half mile, crawling like a spider over the black hills and stopped at an unremarkable gully. It brushed away the heavy rocks with surprising ease, revealing a trapdoor. It spun a circular handle to unlock the door, then opened it. Underneath they found a tunnel and ladder.

"Down here," Porthmeus said unceremoniously before descending headfirst down the ladder, disappearing quickly.

Helesys, Taunauk, and Shawn exchanged weary glances.

Helesys shrugged and offered, "My wand is not giving me warning about the creature, and this is the direction that it wants us to go."

"The wand gives you directions?" Shawn asked.

She nodded. "Not in so many words."

Taunauk added, "It has never steered us wrong."

Shawn glanced from them to the tunnel. "I believe you—both of you. I just hope you guys are looking at the same creepy tunnel I'm looking at. *You* go first, big guy."

"Agreed," he grunted.

Taunauk descended first, holding his axe straight up and down. The passage was just wide enough for him and Everfall, and the shield banged repeatedly on the sides as the barbarian descended. Shawn went next and Helesys went last. Once she was inside, she pulled the hatch down and spun the inner mechanism to lock it, then kindled her wand-arm to light the tunnel.

They descended for what felt like an hour—long enough for Helesys's arms to burn and for confinement to wear on her. She switched hands multiple times to carry the spear and resolved to make a sling for it. She kindled strength, but found her mental fortitude waning. All she could do was tell herself that they had to be close to the bottom.

When they mercifully reached a room that was no more than a giant metal box, Helesys felt numb from empowering herself. The smell of metal and her comrades' musk hung in the air. She dimmed the light from her gauntlet, but it took great, focused effort to slow her breathing and steady herself against the confinement.

Both Taunauk and Shawn also seemed uneasy. The barbarian's arms were flexed and knuckles pale as he clutched the axe tightly. Taunauk stared tentatively at the ceiling, so close he could reach up and touch it. Meanwhile, Shawn was glancing steadily around the room, as if searching for some identifying features.

The current room was perhaps forty feet long, twenty wide, and eight feet high. The walls were slick-faced, showing dappled reflections of the heroes. Hiding their trepidation.

Across the room, Porthmeus was shedding its patchwork cloak, revealing its strange, mechanical body. The whole of it seemed made from the thick silver cords, save for solid plates that went across its chest and back, giving a vaguely Terran outline across the shoulders. Further complicating the illusion was a second pair of arms below the first that had been tucked carefully along its sides.

Once the cloak was shed, Porthmeus's second set of arms unfolded, and the creature resumed its crawling around the floor and walls, looking like a thin bodied spider. As it traced a path along the surfaces, light began to glow from beneath the metal, as if glowing wires were embedded beneath the surface. Neither Porthmeus nor the heroes said anything while the creature completed its alien ritual.

When it finished, the room was awash in steady blue light. If the patterns were runes or writing of some sort, her wand-arm did not translate them.

Porthmeus turned from its strange ritual to the heroes. It half stood, half clung to the nearest wall with three arms, leaving one hand hanging limp by its side.

Again, its beady eyes flitted between them and the silence drug on.

"So, what was all that about?" Shawn asked.

"Sanctity. Solitude. Preparation. *Welcome preparations*," it corrected. "Few guests. Few seek Cogheart."

Helesys asked, "Are you Cogheart?"

"Not anymore. I am anathema. Outcast. Forgotten-One."

Taunauk's grip on his axe audibly relaxed. He replied, "We are Taunauk, Helesys, and Shawn. I am an outcast. Sent away from my tribe and to complete a task I cannot remember. Porthmeus, why are you an outcast?"

"Because I did not want to be Cogheart. Because I am Porthmeus and did not join with the *One-Mind*." When Porthmeus uttered the word, *One-Mind*, its voice grew deep and harsh, then returned to normal. "If you seek the Cogheart, you seek *One-Mind*."

Helesys pointed to the patterns on the walls. "Are you talking to One-Mind?"

"Yes," Porthmeus said. "I am asking permission for you to enter the tunnels. Not sure if *One-Mind* will answer."

Shawn asked, "How long should it take to open—"

A door opened behind Porthmeus—two rectangular halves slid apart with oiled silence, revealing a dark, narrow hallway beyond.

"It is open now," Porthmeus said. It punctuated the statement with an ill-timed sweep of its free hand.

Shawn chuckled nervously and ran a hand over his wispy hair and mumbled, "It's a damn spookshow in here… Not a fan."

Helesys put her elven hand on her friend's shoulder to still him. Her wand-arm was ushering her forward, down the dark hall. In comparison to prior realms, Helesys swore she could feel the wand pulsing beneath the metal, as if it might leap out from its confines and wander the hall of its own accord.

There was something down there, deep underground. A singular thing.

Taunauk eyed her gauntlet and asked, "What do you feel?"

"Direction. Gods, I think I can feel One-Mind." She turned to Porthmeus and asked, "Is that what I'm feeling?"

"Likely; there is nothing else."

Helesys glanced to her comrades, eager to be on her way. "Porthmeus, I think this is where we take our leave." Neither Taunauk nor Shawn offered a counter, though Shawn did not look pleased to be going further inside. He looked more like he was staring down a large, venomous, and ugly predator.

"Be careful," Porthmeus commanded, its eyes settling on Helesys. "You have a long way to go before you reach the core. There are many Cogheart, but they are all parts of *One-Mind.*

Guards, miners, communication nodes, disposal, reconnaissance. All have limited faculties. Minimal conversation potential.

"First layer of One-Mind's bunker is heavily fortified. Numerous guards. Areas of heavy mining. Additional layers are specialized: Furnaces, generators, heat shedding, communication pathways. Information is... outdated. Apologies. *One-Mind* has built additional layers and technology since this one was outcast. No map. No help."

"That's okay," Helesys told the creature. "You have been help enough. We will see ourselves through."

"Wait," Shawn said. "Why would the *thing* let us in to talk to us, but then still order its guards to attack us anyway? That doesn't make sense."

"They are too far away," Porthmeus replied. "*One-Mind* has gone so deep that it struggles to reach Cogheart in the outer layers. They can only obey simple instructions. Guards defend the perimeter. You must make it past them and reach *One-Mind* in the core.

"But even the interior layers will not be safe. There are hunter-killers that patrol the other layers... They are aptly named. Be vigilant." Porthmeus skittered to the floor and to the other side of the double doors, as if allowing them to pass.

Helesys and Shawn stepped forward, but turned when Taunauk did not move.

Taunauk asked, "Are there any others like you?"

"There are no others like me," Porthmeus replied.

"No other outcasts?" the barbarian asked again.

"Clarification: There are other free Cogheart. We all live above the bunker—must live above ground. Others with personalities separate from *One-Mind*. There are no others like me."

Porthmeus's speech had been flat throughout their conversation, but there was a spark of something as it uttered the words *there are no others like me*. Upon hearing the phrase twice, the weaver was sure of it; perhaps a hint of pride.

Helesys eyed her wand-arm curiously and mused on the similar design between it and the creature. Her thoughts drifted to the other made-things encountered in their journeys—Lull, Perdita and the other villagers in the Wode, Amadeus's various guards, the jade lemur in her pocket, Porthmeus, and her wand-arm. All so different, yet stained with magic. All were strange things in an impossible world.

"Why are you helping us?" Helesys asked quietly. The question didn't matter, yet it slipped out.

Porthmeus shook its head—the first time it had moved its head in such a way. "Don't remember. Old instructions, maybe."

Helesys nodded in thanks and Porthmeus returned the Terran gesture.

The weaver kindled her light, and Taunauk led them past the Cogheart and into the dark hall.

"Farewell," Porthmeus said. Helesys couldn't tell if the hint of melancholy in Porthmeus's voice was real or imagined.

The double doors slid shut behind them, taking with them the blue glow and the lone Cogheart.

~ ~ ~

First Layer

They continued down the narrow hall. Even with her light dim, Helesys's gauntlet casted harsh shadows from between her comrades. The walls, floor, and ceiling showed a muddled reflection of the three as they walked. The surfaces were smooth, but vague shadows of lines or piping could be seen if she held the light close.

The elf weaver looked between her comrades, noting that both walked stiffer than usual. "Perhaps I should lead," she said plainly. "This place has you both on edge."

Taunauk glanced at the walls. "It is tighter here than I would like. Little room to move." He rolled his shoulders and hoisted his shield and axe for effect, the blade rapping against the metal. There wouldn't be enough room for him to fight as he was accustomed too. There was scarcely enough room for Taunauk to walk normally.

Behind her, Shawn added, "I think it's the combination. You know, first it was the inhospitable landscape. Now it's the underground, tight spaces, and creepy, killer automatons. Yep, let's go with all of that."

Helesys said, "Porthmeus said Cogheart in the lower realms could be reasoned with."

"But not the ones here," Shawn added quietly. "We're on the perimeter and still haven't seen any guards yet."

"Quiet," Taunauk whispered. "There's a junction up ahead."

The barbarian led them silently to the first such branching path and peered carefully down each of the three new halls. Again, Helesys felt the guidance of her wand-arm. It was telling them to turn right.

Just as she pointed to the right, she felt danger from directly ahead.

"Our path leads to the right, but we have enemies coming from ahead of us." Helesys leaned back against the wall, churned power and leveled her gauntlet—ready for whatever was coming. Taunauk stepped forward, blocking the hall with his body and the ironwood shield.

"What is it?" Shawn said, trying to peer around his comrades. "What do you see?"

From down the hall came a mass of twisted silver and flashing blue lights. Crawling spiders in the shape of Porthmeus, undulating worms, and buzzing winged insects. They poured down the hall like floodwaters.

"A swarm," Taunauk said. "Run!"

Shawn took off down the right hall. Helesys pushed Taunauk to the side and fired three quick blasts before following. Taunauk was right behind her.

Down the hall, the blasts collided with the swarm with mangled screeches of metal. Still, the swarm came. It turned the corner and followed them. The buzzing and scratching of metal wings and claws grew louder.

Helesys kindled speed and the sleek hall passed around her like she was flying. Shawn was stopped up ahead at the next junction.

"Helesys, which way!" the rogue shouted.

The weaver sighed—she couldn't tell from so far away. She looked back over her shoulder and fired three more blasts. Neither she nor Taunauk slowed to watch.

She was only steps away when she knew the direction for certain. "Straight ahead!"

Helesys slowed at the junction, then kindled power and the Ring of Winter. She let loose two charged blasts—one directly at the swarm and the other at the corner of the intersection. The first icy blast collided with the mass of insect-like automatons, clumping them together and spreading easily through the mass of metal. The second hit the corner of the junction and spread similarly up the walls, completely blocking the passage with opaque ice.

The elf turned to keep running at speed and nearly ran Shawn over. The rogue ran beside her, both trying to catch the barbarian who was down the tunnel.

"That ring has come in quite handy," Shawn said. "Just remember to keep it at a length from me."

"I haven't forgotten," Helesys replied coyly. "Neither elf nor human, but can't handle the cold."

He shrugged. "I was made for the beach."

Taunauk was paused at the next junction. Helesys kept running and trying to sense what direction to go next, without willing to slow her speed. Nor could she see around Taunauk's bulk. So it wasn't until she stumbled over her feet and into him that she realized their path went downward—

The pair fell forward into a sloping chute and quickly picked up speed.

Shawn was behind them, screaming wildly in amusement.

~

The slick metal of the chute gave way to a rocky cavern and the three heroes fell to a pile of rubble and tumbled down the face of it. Helesys, Taunauk, and Shawn slid to a stop and looked upon a large cavern. It stretched off into the distance, veins of rock glowing the same eerie blue as the metal halls, the curves of it looking nearly natural. The walls and rocks around them were all the deep black as those above ground, but they had been worn smooth. Each shift of Helesys's weight sent cascades of the smooth stones down the hill.

The cavern was filled with such piles of stones. The weaver slid down the rest of the pile, joining Taunauk and Shawn on the ground.

"An abandoned mine?" Helesys said idly.

"Looks to be," Shawn replied.

"We cannot stay here," Taunauk said, eyeing their surroundings. "Too open."

The barbarian was right. They were better off in the halls where the swarm could be funneled. In the open, they would be easily overwhelmed.

From the chute opening above them, sharp cracks sounded—the swarm was breaking through the ice. Helesys kindled power and ice and fired again, sealing the opening of the chute as best she could.

The weaver focused on her wand-arm, but down there she had only a vague sense of direction—as if the depth or the open space hampered her wand. She pointed across the cavern and the three took off running again. They skirted mound after mound of smooth stones, gaping boreholes that dropped into darkness, and giant digging machines with scoops each big enough to lift a giant and chain links taller than Taunauk. The giant machines were still, half-full of rubble and half-buried—as if they'd been abandoned in the middle of their task.

Then they passed a slanted hole, one with tiny spider-like automatons still using it. The robots were no bigger than a hand, with dark spiral shells on their backs. The shells of the ones going into the holes glowed a fierce blue.

Immediately, Helesys felt direction from her wand-arm. "Down there," she said, pointing down the slope.

Cracks sounded in the distance—from the chute Helesys had frozen over. Then an explosion burst from the hole, ice and smoke and a flash of flame. The swarm poured out and crawled along the ceiling. Silver and blue covered the ceiling, spreading like a puddle. None touched the floor at first, but the flying automatons began diving to the ground and exploding. Each crash echoed across the cavern, quaking the heaps of stone. Getting steadily closer.

The three heroes crouched behind the borehole wall.

"They don't know where we are," Shawn said. "They're searching for us."

"Let's make them wait a little longer," Taunauk said. "Come."

They took off running again. Supernatural speed and a downhill slope culminated with Helesys feeling as if she was flying down the borehole. She kindled a small light with her gauntlet, but channeled the rest to strength and speed, pushing away the dull burn in her legs. Her strides grew long on the slope, until she was hurtling down it, flying ten feet with every step. Shawn and Taunauk did likewise, until the three were skipping like stones along the surface, cloaks fluttering madly behind them. The blue lights of the stream of automatons became a blur.

~

Helesys lost track of how long they ran. The borehole seemed endless, as if they were running to the center of the realm. The dull burn in her legs was sharp now despite the kindled strength and endurance from her wand. Her left arm was cramped from holding the Gar of Shéslang.

But they dared not stop. Explosions sounded from behind them and pinpricks of light flashed in the distance. The swarm was after them. Gaining on them.

Helesys's mind slipped back to the deck of the *Malorienta*, to when she had blasted falling rocks during their passage through the cliffs. When she slipped into a trance that took her back to the great halls of her life before—to losing herself in dance.

As they sprinted across the downward slope, Helesys's strides had grown gigantic. Bounding instead of running. So she began to time her steps and with every third she leapt even higher than normal, spinning in the air and loosing repeating blasts from her wand-arm and the Ring of Winter. Icy blasts soared up the tunnel toward the distant swarm.

"Look at you!" Shawn shouted. "Gotta get me one of those."

Helesys smirked but kept up the pace.

Taunauk kept glancing back toward the swarm with a stoic expression on his face. "They're gaining on us."

"Oh ho, look at that!" Shawn shouted.

A ripple of water appeared in the distance and grew rapidly.

"Whatever it is," Helesys said, "it has to be better than the swarm."

It looked like a glowing blue pond and another immense cavern. The spiral-shelled miners were converging and diving beneath the surface.

Again hoping to put distance between themselves and the swarm, Helesys ceased firing and instead channeled the full might of the Ring of Winter. She felt the tendril of cold slide out from her finger, feeling a stabbing along the nerves in her left arm, but she concentrated and held fast to the Gar of Shéslang.

The god-serpent had called the spear a conduit—something that would help her channel magical power. It was time to put that to the test.

The next time Helesys leapt, she channeled the ring and spun the spear, making several revolutions as she soared. The tendril of winter lashed itself to the length of the weapon, the shard of bright white lengthened until it touched the wall of the borehole.

She felt the words of power come to her, dredged from some arcane depth. "*Murum glaciei tempestatemque.*"

In a single fantastic surge, cold seeped forth from the tendril and ice grew from where it touched the metal. In one final circle, ice burst from the outer wall of the tunnel, crystals growing until they reached the center, and interlocking to make a wall of ice.

Helesys touched down on the borehole without missing a step and felt cold seep around her. Frost colored the metal surface and misty breath trailed from her lips. She felt the tendril of the ring retreating, diminished from use.

Taunauk and Shawn were beside her, bounding down the passage—smirk of satisfaction on the barbarian's face and disbelief on the rogue's.

Both were short-lived, as explosions sounded behind them.

All they needed was a little time.

The last stretch of the tunnel grew warm and slick with steam. It opened to the immense cavern, the centerpiece of which was the glowing blue pond. It was unbearably warm and sweat immediately began beading on Helesys's forehead.

Helesys waved them to follow and on numb legs, they ran around the rocky shore of the pond toward the other end of the cavern. The weaver's gauntlet led them to a small hidden door built into the black rock.

"*Stercus,*" Shawn said, "How do we open it?"

Cracks echoed from the borehole.

Helesys could feel the warding magic over the door, keeping it shut. "Give me a moment."

Behind, Taunauk and Shawn turned to face the tunnel and the coming swarm. More cracks, tearing. Not long.

Helesys pressed her metal hand to the door, searching the embedded magic as she searched for seams between realms, searching for the words as she did at the gates of Shéslang. When the words came to her, she spoke them aloud. "*By frozen warmth and captured dream, reveal to us thy hidden scheme. Permit us entry, and thine secrets we shall redeem.*"

Explosions now—the swarm was through the frozen barricade.

The double doors slid open with quiet resignation, and Helesys and the others stepped inside.

The swarm slowly poured into the cavern—with none of the speed and urgency expected of it. Helesys watched as hundreds of blue lights—of eyes—turned toward the heroes. The swarm merely watched as the double doors shut.

~ ~ ~

Second Layer

The heroes backed away from the door, weapons ready, but were met with only silence.

Helesys blasted the door anyway, sealing it with a meager amount of ice. She had tapped the limits Ring of Winter, and she was weary to push them further—lest overuse cause irreparable damage to it or to her.

Beside her, Shawn sighed heavily and relaxed his guard. "What's all that about? Why did they let us go? Not that I mind," he added in between breaths. "Breath to fate, and all that."

Helesys already knew the answer, Taunauk merely gave voice to it.

The barbarian was already staring off down the hall, axe still in hand and at the ready. "Guards patrol the outer layers. We must have passed through the first layer. Porthmeus said there were others… hunter-killers. Keep your guard up."

The hallway in front of them was not the same as before. Its walls and floor were split and unlevel, as if thick piping or cables ran beneath the surface. The surfaces themselves were smooth and seamless, but flowed and pooled in sections like sagging skin, like the walls had melted and resolidified. Even the blue glow emanating from the walls seemed warped and wavering.

"I suggest we switch our marching order," Shawn whispered. When Helesys and Taunauk both looked to him with questions, the rogue added, "I am the quietest of us. Stay a dozen paces behind me. Taunauk, perhaps you should stay in the rear, in case one of those hunters decides to flank us. Either way, Helesys has sight from the middle." He turned to Helesys. "I'll wait for you at the junctions."

After some hesitation, Taunauk pulled Everfall from his back and nodded. "*This* time."

~

Shawn led them through the warped tunnels and mottled darkness. Helesys and Taunauk followed.

The tunnels stretched on in a crisscrossing maze. Every one hundred feet or so, they came to a four-way junction. Shawn paused at each junction, signaled for his comrades to follow, then waited for them to catch up. Inevitably, one of the directions was on a slight decline, leading further down to the core of the underground; that was always the direction Helesys's wand-arm ushered them.

At first, Taunauk seemed reserved about letting the rogue lead. Taunauk was accustomed to being the shield and spear-tip of the group to Helesys's archer. The barbarian was also considerably stealthy—moving with the quiet of a jungle cat. But to the rogue's credit, Shawn moved with the silence of a specter. Twice, Helesys glanced behind her, past Taunauk, only to return and find that Shawn was across the tunnel in that same breath. She had never seen someone move so silently *and* so quickly. She had no doubt that the rogue fared well on his solitary journeys—whole realms never realizing that he had passed silently beside them.

~

During one stretch, the right side of the hallway opened up to a massive underground lake—as if an explosion or mining had peeled away the walls. Huge black towers rose out of the clear water and up through the cavern ceiling. Shimmers of heat radiated from the towers where they touched open air, but the room felt temperate.

Helesys paused at the sight—feeling a tug of familiarity. The rogue and barbarian stopped wearily beside her.

"Let's rest," Taunauk said. "This place is as good as any."

The barbarian led them out of the hallway and to the side of a small outcropping of black hills. Helesys sat to the left, Shawn to the middle, and Taunauk on the side closest to the hallway opening. They sat down wearily, pulled rations from their packs and shared jerky.

Helesys felt the sharp burn of exhaustion in her legs and the salt of the jerky, but she was staring at the towers. Finally, realization dawned on her. "These are the heat shedding that Porthmeus spoke of. Those towers lead down to furnaces. They use water to cool them."

"How do you know that?" Shawn asked.

The weaver looked to her wand-arm, flexing the pointed metallic fingers. "More than once, someone has commented on the magic of the elves. I think… I *feel* that my people had similar technology. Maybe even a similar scale. It echoes with me," she added. Taunauk took her reference.

Shawn said curiously, "I didn't know the elves would be so… *unnatural* in their architecture."

Helesys said, "Perhaps you spent more time with humans rather than elves."

The rogue smiled sullenly and nodded. "I remember a village, near a factory reminiscent of this one. It belched smoke into the air. Soot lined the street and crept into the houses. I lived there, at least for a time, with a human grandfather and granddaughter. They took me in… Movernus knows why… I can't imagine you elves wanted to live near such a thing."

"I imagine one gets used to it," Helesys replied.

"The world changes around the Terran," Taunauk mused. "Then the world changes them."

"I suppose the barbarian's stay far from such things," Shawn said slyly.

Taunauk shrugged. "One Terran's barbarism is another's comfort."

Helesys added, "One religion's worship is another's blasphemy."

Shawn waved a hand. "Yes, yes, and one holds the pommel while the enemy stares down the blade of the same dagger."

Helesys smirked.

Taunauk patted Shawn on the back. "Well said. We will make a philosopher of you yet."

~

They rested long enough to eat and stretch, and only a few minutes more. Then continued through the halls, descending with every junction. The ridges and hidden wires continued along the walls, as did the occasional melted segments. Despite the group's steady progress, the direction from Helesys's wand-arm grew no more potent.

Perhaps it was a trick of the confines or they simply were so very far away from the core—either way, Helesys tried not to let worry show on her face. She tried to focus on the steady progression. Focused only on the hallway in front of her and the hallway behind her.

"Wait," Taunauk whispered.

Helesys froze beside him.

The barbarian was staring back the way they came, watching their flank. He switched to hold both the Everfall shield and axe with his left hand, then knelt and placed his right palm flat on the floor.

Helesys said nothing. She kindled power in her wand-arm and glanced down the hall to Shawn, who was already at the next junction.

The rogue stopped, too. He slipped to the left corner and crouched, holding his hand out in a "wait" signal.

"Something is following us," Taunauk whispered.

"Two somethings," Helesys replied. "Shawn, up ahead."

"Shit!" Shawn whisper-yelled. "What the shit!"

From down the hall, Helesys heard the harsh scraping of metal on metal, constant and whirring, like a sword across a grindstone.

Shawn backed around the corner of the hall and drew twin daggers, one white and the other black and jagged.

Then the same ominous scraping echoed from the other hall, near her and Taunauk. The barbarian rose and readied his weapons. Helesys stepped away, distancing herself from Taunauk, eyes flitting between both ends of the hall and gauntlet humming with anticipation.

A metal spider-like thing rounded the corner of Shawn's hall, but Helesys didn't have time to stare before a second she heard sounds behind her. She turned just in time to see the second one collide with Taunauk's shield with a thunderous clang.

They were far from the swarm of creatures they had met above—these were the hunter-killers that Porthmeus warned of.

The metal creature had a thick serpent-like body roughly fifteen feet long, blue lights flashing along its length. It had two limbs at each end, each limb ending with a triangular-shaped blade. The headless automaton clung to the wall with three limbs at a time—sliding along the ridges and grooves. It attacked with a single limb at a time, spinning the triangular blade until it whirred viciously.

Taunauk met the spinning blade with Everfall, repelling the creature—testing it. Metal screeched against the ironwood shield, but the barbarian held his ground. He slashed with the battleaxe, but the hunter-killer spun from the walls to the ceiling, rotating over itself, switching its clinging hands and attacking hand as it did, like a dancer pivoting during a routine. Taunauk grunted in frustration.

Helesys fired two staggered bursts over Taunauk's head—the hallway was too narrow to chance shooting around his sides. If anything, she could deny the hunter-killer its vertical motion and level the battleground.

Behind her, Shawn fought an identical foe using speed instead of brawn. The automaton was a frenzy of blades and blue. It spun from ceiling to wall to floor, trying to catch the rogue. Shawn was a blur, leaping and twisting, slipping over and under the spinning blade. But all his focus was on evasion; Helesys couldn't see him lashing out with either dagger.

She couldn't risk firing at Shawn's attacker, for their speed was too much to follow and she did not want to hit Shawn on accident.

So often she had relied on the sheer power of her arcane blasts, on the advantage that attacking at range provided. But now the narrow hallways were *her disadvantage*. Instead of bottlenecking the automatons, they had bottlenecked the heroes. Briefly, she thought of the Ring of Winter. That she might cast it on the metal walls to freeze the hunter-killers in place. But the power of the ring was low, and there was no guarantee that she could do so without compromising her comrades' footing. She could turn her magic to countering the strength and speed of the hunter-killers, but she could feel no magic powering them—whatever power they had, it was not something that she could take away so easily.

Helesys was stuck between two frenzied battles, for the first time feeling the limits of her arcane might—wondering how she could fight in such confines when there was scarcely enough room for Taunauk or Shawn.

The one comfort was that Taunauk's situation was not dire enough to warrant his golden, fiery glow. Shawn's on the other hand...

What if she could bolster her allies instead?

Helesys rested the butt of the spear on the metal floor and grasped it with both hands. The weaver closed her eyes and concentrated. Instead of reaching out into the ether as she did when opening the seams, Helesys concentrated on the sounds of battle. In the darkness, she heard and felt the clash of weapons, and then the steps and breath of her allies.

In the darkness, the weaver swore that *she could see*.

"*Amplificare potentia*."

Just as Helesys felt the seams, she felt her comrades. She felt as if she were looking over their shoulders—No—She felt as if she *were* them, as if she were living their steps, feeling the impact of shield and dagger, rise and fall of their chests.

In Taunauk, she felt power as she had never felt it before. Her bolstered strength or endurance felt insignificant next to a barbarian's. The hunter-killer slashed with inhuman strength and collided with the ironwood shield. A lesser mortal would've shattered, but the outlander stopped it as surely as if he were a bulwark of steel. The impact echoed through his bones, his arms, shoulder and legs, dissipated by sheer strength and generations of barbarian blood magic.

She felt his rage. She felt anger boiling inside him, flooding his muscles with power. Anger of being trapped in the dungeon, of being kept from his home and his tribe, of being denied a barbarian's glorious death in battle, of being exiled and denied the reason why. She felt all of it building to utter fury at this automaton that dared stand in Taunauk's way, that dared prolong his search and his suffering. Taunauk thought of nothing, save for destroying the insolent beast.

Helesys thought back to their deaths in the endless sea at the edge of the realm, back to the boiling surf, the towering crests, and abyssal valleys between waves. Taunauk's rage felt like a bottled storm. His blood boiled, sweat beaded beneath his armor, hot breath and spittle sprayed from his mouth. Everfall and axe were the valleys and crests of waves.

She felt a quiet promise of solace that this enemy's death would placate the barbarian. This automaton's death would be penance for now.

So the weaver gave him a small boon of power—no more than breathing speed into the winds of his storm. But those winds churned the waves to even greater heights and tore open a whirlpool in the sea.

Helesys felt the surge of strength, of crashing axe and shield cracking like a whip or like thunder against the hunter-killer. Shudders of impact as the inhuman metal buckled and twisted beneath the might of the barbarian.

And in the same moment Helesys felt the barbarian, she also felt Shawn. There were two parts to the rogue—the flesh that was as fast as the mouse and as cunning as a cat. The part that prowled and hunted, yet felt mortal fear. Yet there was another part of the rogue, half-hidden even from him, that knew he was untouchable. Shawn felt like the wind—like a breeze that couldn't be caught. He bounded and slipped the hunter-killer's weapons like they were the still-branches of trees.

The contrast between her comrades was impossibly stark— if Taunauk was an ironwood tree or a raging storm, then Shawn was a playful cat or a giggling child.

So Helesys gave him a much larger boon of power. Enough to turn the rogue's playful breeze into a gale that bent saplings and broke branches. The giddiness of his hidden prowess grew, pushing aside mortal fear, moving with reckless abandon. His body was as light as air.

Even though Helesys felt Shawn, she could no longer see him or follow his actions. His movements became impossible to watch, his twists and dodges happening in the space between heartbeats, slashes—faster than blinks. She swore that twice the hunter-killer's blade struck Shawn and phased right through him or his after-image.

Shawn became unshackled by the burdens of flesh. He became the flicker of a half-remembered dream or a desperately forgotten nightmare.

Moments had passed since Helesys's spell. Only moments. But that was enough.

Taunauk broke the arm of his hunter-killer with a bash from Everfall, shearing the arm off at the joint, then his axe fell like a towering wave, slicing clean through the body of the automaton, nearly splitting it in half. Armor plating scattered across the hall and wires sagged from the gaping wound. The hunter-killer crashed limp and lifeless to the floor.

Meanwhile, Shawn had enveloped his automaton in a flurry of daggers. His hunter-killer dropped to the ground, twitching slightly. Its body was a mangled mess, covered with dozens of gashes—looking more like tattered fabric than metal. The light was completely gone from both.

Helesys gasped and relinquished the spell. She dropped to one knee and held the Gar of Shéslang with both hands to keep herself up. Her arms and legs and her chest burned. So potent and focused the spell, that she felt empty and tired—as if she'd forgotten to breathe. The weaver gasped for air and forced herself to stand.

She found her comrades in similar fashion. Taunauk stowed Everfall upon his back, chest heaving. Shawn stowed his daggers, then leaned against the wall of the hallway. He gasped as well, then waved and nodded aimlessly that he was okay.

~

For a long moment, no one moved. Both Shawn and Taunauk watched the halls for more enemies, while Helesys kept power at the ready. When the three of them finally recovered from the battle with the hunter-killers, and it was clear that no more were coming, Taunauk broke the silence.

"You didn't need to do that," the barbarian said.

Helesys stared at her comrade. "I couldn't have helped any other way. I couldn't shoot around you, nor counter—"

"How did you do that?" Taunauk asked, uneasily.

"It was the opposite of countering an opponent's magic. Similar to the magic I use to open the seams between worlds. I felt your abilities, then amplified them."

Shawn interjected, "Well, that was bloody brilliant." The rogue was still breathing heavily, but he no longer needed the support of the wall. He wagged a finger. "Just warn me next time. The come down is rough."

Helesys looked to Taunauk, but the barbarian still looked at her uneasily. "What's the matter?" she asked.

The outlander shook his head. "It was a boon but it felt...wrong."

She asked, "Haven't we spoken at length about using all the tools and gifts at our disposal? Was bolstering your strength so different?"

Taunauk measured his response. "It wasn't my strength you touched. It was my rage. It was the blood-magic of the Endroggen. Something *only* shared between our people and our enemies."

"Then I apologize," she replied, clenching her teeth in frustration. "We have shared memories… I didn't realize my mistake."

The barbarian stared at her, melancholy on his face. "I… I'm sorry too. Were I truly *Aonar*, I would feel differently. But I am not alone—I carry the the spirits of my people. Shéslang said they saw faces and spirits, and I know now that they *must be* Endroggen."

Helesys's annoyance subsided. Of course, Taunauk had a reason for denying her magic—was it so different from after her struggles against the blue Terrans in the cavern of

Shéslang? She nearly swore to keep her memories from him, from one of the only two people she could trust in this world.

She merely replied, "I understand. I shall support you in other ways." She resolved to let the outlander come to terms with his ethereal passengers on his own.

"I think I understand too," Shawn said quietly, walking over to the both of them. "That was too... I suppose, *intimate*, would be the word. No apology necessary. It's just... I felt what the Voice on the Beach was talking about. I'm not completely Terran. I've definitely got something else going on, if you know what I mean."

Helesys merely nodded. She had also felt the two distinct parts of Shawn. She added idly, "Almost as if you're one of the spirits that follows Taunauk."

Shawn pondered that a moment before smiling candidly. "Perhaps when we make it to the Godpeak, the spirits can give me insight, too. They know everything, right?"

Helesys and Taunauk shared a grin and felt the mood lighten.

"We will ask them together," Taunauk replied. "But first, the Cogheart."

~

The heroes' journey took them further into the depths of One-Minds's bunker. They descended ten more junctions in tense silence and peace before coming to another cavern cut away from the hall.

Helesys's gauntlet directed them through the cavern, and the weaver, barbarian, and rogue stalked through it.

Heat billowed through the sprawling cavern. Again, Helesys saw great mounds, but this time made of scrap metal instead of rock and rubble. In the piles, she could make out dull spiral shells, long twisted cables, and arms and bodies that might've been hunter-killers. They stuck close to these lifeless piles as they walked through.

The familiar rock walls hung above them, but the floor between the mounds of rubble was filled with a fine gray dirt. The entirety of the cavern seemed to glow with the same blue light that permeated the halls and the rest of the structure, except that now it seemed to come from the piles.

At one point, Shawn stooped down to a thin piece of wire that lay by itself and inspected it. Then he tossed it onto a nearby pile of rubbish. As soon as the wire landed, it began to glow with the same blue light as surely as if it had caught fire.

"Woah," Shawn whispered, patting his pockets and taking a measured step back from the pile.

"Indeed," Helesys added. The weaver held out her metal hand to sense for magic and careful to give the other metal a wide berth. She felt a kindling of magic, something reminiscent of the rotting magic she learned a half-dozen deaths ago in the Wode—the magic that so easily destroyed the birchmen. Subtle heat, too, emanated from the piles; likely a byproduct of the magic.

She said quietly, "It is magic meant to break down the garbage. Like a slow-burning flame." She pushed around the fine dirt with the toe of her boot. "There aren't any rocks here. I think we're standing on top of a rotted, broken down metal."

"Funny creature, this One-Mind," Shawn said.

Taunauk grunted thoughtfully. "Breaking down metal to remake it as something new. Like a smithery turning metal into a blade or a forest growing from the dead."

"Now that doesn't..." Shawn started to say, before trailing off and looking around him and back the way they came—as if seeing the underground facility completely anew. Finally, he put his hands on his hips and shrugged. "That is certainly an interesting way of looking at it."

Helesys smiled, for she agreed; it *was* an eloquent way of looking at it—from an outlander, no less. Taunauk had seen it before she had, before the elf whose people were more acquainted with such technology.

Rather than dwell on the insight, Taunauk merely waved with his shield for them to continue.

They crossed the cavern in much the same marching order as before: Shawn slinking carefully ahead, then waving for Helesys and Taunauk to continue. Helesys and Taunauk stayed closer together, ready for whatever threat might lurk around the corner, be it a hunter-killer or something else.

The cavern stretched on, and it wasn't until they had been walking for hours more that they came to something different—

A pile of scrap, no higher than the rest, but that glowed with red lights instead of blue. Rather than a glow emanating from all the surfaces, the red lights glowed in patches. As they walked closer, Helesys could feel the heat emanating from the patches, so hot that the metals were melting and deforming in and around the glow.

The weaver's mouth fell agape, for in the pile, she saw skulls and bones littered throughout. Terran and animal.

Shawn pulled out his white dagger and poked at the ground nearby. "Teeth," he mumbled. Helesys looked down and saw them littering the ground, like ashen shells upon a beach.

Her gauntlet hummed with warning—but not from the grotesque pile. It was growing stronger, as if danger was approaching.

"Hide. Quick," she whispered.

She, Taunauk, and Shawn slipped behind the nearest blue pile of metal, both crouched tentatively behind it and careful not to touch the pile itself.

From across the cavern sounded the sliding of oiled steel and soft thumps of dozens of legs upon the ground. Helesys could see around Shawn's shoulder, and she was vaguely aware of Taunauk peering around her as well.

Between the piles walked a procession of hunter-killers, glowing red instead of blue. Their legs, that before had been triangular and rotating, were now unfurled and piercing the ground like the many legs of a devilish centipede—each triangle having become two separate blades.

Helesys slipped carefully to the other side of their mound in an attempt to count the number of enemies, but saw she...

The leading hunter-killer had a face. Its first two arms were holding the blades or legs in front of it, with the triangles rearranged to form two eyes and a mouth. The other hunter-killers were not a procession—here multiple automatons should've begun and ended, Helesys saw only a single long torso, at least six lengths of the hunter-killers they fought before. Instead of smooth steel, the length of the torso was covered in twisted plates, cable, skulls and bones.

The giant automaton marched over to the red pile of molten scrap, then walked a circle around it. The legs on the inside brushed at the pile as if the creature was tidying up the stack. Its last two sets of legs came into view, dragging the limp remains of a separate hunter-killer.

The giant creature encircled the pile completely. When its head had walked around and met its back end, the giant unfurled its face back into arms and began slicing and tearing at the derelict hunter-killer. Squeals of tearing, twisting metal filled the cavern. Some pieces were torn off and hurled into the pile, others were ripped off and tossed into the molten red patches.

Shawn tapped Helesys on the shoulder, startling her. The rogue gestured over his shoulder that they should "move on".

Helesys and Taunauk agreed, and the three of them slunk away and around several piles.

She was about to breathe a sigh of relief when she heard a rumble echo through the cavern, so strong she felt it through the silty floor.

"Halt."

All three heroes turned and saw the glaring metal face of the giant hunter-killer. It was perched on top of its red mound, top half standing upright in the air like a serpent, towering over the cavern. A pair of arms hung limp at its sides, the full length of the blades were menacing.

More vibrations rumbled through the ground and Helesys's wand-arm translated—turning them into words. Each re-sounded with a metallic clang, like the stroke of a blacksmith's hammer.

"My name is Dissimul and you are trespassing."

"Is it talking?" Shawn whispered, not taking his eyes off the automaton.

Helesys merely nodded and knelt. She placed the palm of her metal hand to the ground and spoke back with her own rumbling. *"We seek passage to One-Mind. This one has questions."* She stared at the abstract face perched atop the mound... waiting.

Shawn crouched, as if unsure whether he was supposed to kneel before the creature. Taunauk merely stood, axe and Everfall already in hand.

Moments passed in tense silence and grew foreboding.

Helesys spoke again. "*We are Helesys, Taunauk, and Shawn. We have questions for One-Mind, and then we will leave this realm.*"

Of all the creatures she had spoken to—men and monsters and gods—none was as tense as speaking to Dissimul. All others have some measure of wants, needs, and purpose. If this hunter-killer was like the others, then it should've attacked her. And as the moments of silence dragged on, Helesys didn't grow hopeful. She grew suspicious.

Finally, Dissimul rumbled and spoke. "*I have heard many languages. Shouts, gasps, whispers. Most spoken in terror—none that I understood. I have never heard another speak my own language. This is… unexpected.*" The massive automaton remained unmoved.

"*You do not speak the language of One-Mind?*" Helesys asked. "*Does it not speak the same tongue?*"

"*No,*" the hunter-killer replied. "*One-Mind does not speak to me.*"

Shawn lowered himself to one knee and Taunauk knelt tentatively on the other side of her, both awaiting her signal, should she give it.

Helesys said, "*We could speak to One-Mind on your behalf. As a sign of gratitude for safe passage.*"

"*You will not speak to One-Mind about me.*"

The weaver grit her teeth in frustration. "*What boon can we offer for passage?*"

"*The two others do not speak. How are you speaking to me?*"

"*I am a weaver. I am using magic.*"

Dissimul said, "*I do not see your wand.*"

She hesitated—the subtle hum of warning from the wand in her forearm was growing. Helesys said, "*I have a wand. What boon can we offer for passage?*"

The giant hunter-killer slunk down from its molten red pile. It walked backwards, giving the appearance that its head was sinking into the rubbish.

Shawn and Taunauk rose quickly. The barbarian raised his shield, while the rogue drew his black dagger and another silver one, large and curved like a sickle.

"Stercus," Helesys cursed. "Get ready."

"*You shall not pass,*" Dissimul said as it disappeared behind the piles. "*In the name of the One-Mind, I sentence you to Un-Making.*"

The rumble of the automaton's speech was replaced with tremors as the giant hunter-killer weaved through the piles of rubble toward them.

"On with it then!" Taunauk roared.

The barbarian stepped forward defiantly, half-crouched behind his shield and with axe half-raised. Shawn slunk back and to the right until he was behind the nearest mound of scrap. Helesys stepped backward to the left, far enough from both— should she need Taunauk's protection or need to draw Dissimul's attention from Shawn's ambush.

Helesys kindled both strength and power. She had seen enough of the hunter-killers' speed in the tunnels that she would not be caught unaware in the open. As strength and speed flooded her muscles, she siphoned the rest of her power into her gauntlet. The comforting hum of power grew to a rattle—and her bolstered strength would be all the better at handling the recoil.

Meanwhile, the Gar of Shéslang grew warmer in her left hand. Helesys had only ever felt the pull and draw of her gauntlet… and the subtle touch of another magic item surprised her. Her arm gave direction and warning, and translated for her. The spear… felt bold, as if it *wanted* battle. Helesys smirked, for the spear had been stuck in the hide of the god Shéslang—the god who had bore through rock and earth and caused incredible destruction in the earlier moments of its birth. Perhaps the weapon retained some of the god's latent destruction.

Thoughts and the smirk both left Helesys as the giant hunter-killer thundered around the corner. Dissimul sprinted toward them, legs piercing the ground like the frenzied stabs of battalion pikes. The abstract face unfurled to its front limbs—four blades that slid against each other like the mandibles of a spider.

"*Foghar siorruidh!*" Taunauk shouted. A veil of autumn leaves burst from Everfall and swirled in the air around the barbarian.

Dissimul slammed into Taunauk, and a horrid crunch echoed through the cavern. Taunauk was pushed back, his heels sliding through the dirt and just appearing from behind the veil of leaves before the magic encircled him again. Clangs of impact and squeals of metal echoed from within, the arc of Taunauk's axe and Dissimul's pistoning blades just peering out from the swirl of reds, oranges, and yellows.

While the head fought the barbarian, the horrid length of the automaton was snaking its way over the left most pile of scrap. As it walked over the mound, the spear-like legs left red blotches of light behind—as if they were polluting the light of the One-Mind. The body continued to swing around as if it meant to encircle Taunauk and attack his flank.

Helesys braced herself and fired a barrage of arcane power at the back-half of the creature. The purple blasts collided with the mottled armor, tearing chunks of plate and wire from it.

Suddenly, Shawn leapt to the back of the automaton—having circled around behind it. The rogue held fast where the nape of its neck might have been, taking advantage of Taunauk's distraction to attack the slender body itself. Within moments, Dissimul reached backward with two pairs of its claw-blades, stabbing at the rogue to force him away. But Shawn slipped around like an insect, and the great automaton likely caused more damage to itself with its own misguided blades.

With its attention divided, Dissimul could not effectively fight all three. The giant hunter-killer began to undulate its body, rising and thrashing in attempt to avoid Helesys's blasts and to throw the rogue off its back.

But none of the heroes relented. Armor, wire, finally sparks flew from the beast as Helesys's gauntlet tore through its back half and Shawn sunk his daggers into it. For a moment, it looked as if their victory was assured.

Then Dissimul's face formed on the other end—at the end that Helesys was fighting. The two sullen eyes and mouth stared at her.

Helesys paused, wand-arm still trained on the creature and simmering with heat—the front half of it still writhing and fighting her two comrades. Red light ebbed from beneath its armor as if the automaton was bleeding.

Dissimul charged at her, thundering across the battlefield. Its back end was now its front, and again she felt the rumble of speech through the ground.

"Weaver! I'll tear the wand from your arm!"

The weaver sapped power from her wand-arm and bolstered her strength and speed as much as she could. Her arms and legs grew tight, as if they were straining at the fabric of her clothes or the muscle fibers were straining at her skin. She crouched and felt like a panther. Her chest heaved deep with the breath of a warhorse. She squeezed both hands on the Gar of Shéslang, and she felt the spear's quiet yearning for battle.

The hunter-killer's face unfurled to four bladed-arms as it descended on her.

Helesys dodged backward, diving, rolling, twisting and ducking beneath the blades as the end of the beast passed over her, but even as it passed by, each subsequent pair of limbs lashed out at her. Still, the weaver slipped each vicious swing with kindled might.

The end of Dissimul turned round and swooped back toward her like a bird of prey.

Again, she felt the yearning of the spear—a humble request for use. So, Helesys obliged it. She split her power between her body and the Gar of Shéslang. The warm metal grew hot and violent, and when the abomination came for her, instead of retreating, Helesys lashed out.

She met the blades of Dissimul with the bolstered strength and magic imbued spear. Clangs and squeals of metal rang out. The impacts shuddered through her arms and Helesys gasped with pain and surprise—had her muscles and bones not been reinforced with magic, they would've no doubt shattered. A dozen blows exchanged in an instant—for every two slashes she parried, Helesys struck back another.

The weaver was taken back to the deck of the *Malorienta*, to her dance of destruction as the ship passed through the narrows. To the memories of dancing in the Great Hall. Memories came to her unbidden again, spurred on by battle and desperation. But this time, they were not the carefree memories of dance, but memories of the Eternal Battlefield. Of blastshells and destruction and death.

Helesys had known she was a soldier—even before any memories of such had come back to her. Just as the mechanical abomination in front of her was made with a singular purpose, Helesys felt that she was too. She relinquished herself, giving into the ease of violence. To anger. She thought of Taunauk's rage—how the boiling of power and emotion felt.

She was only vaguely aware of the thrashing automaton. Of Taunauk and Shawn leaping onto its back. Taunauk was aglow with shimmering light, and sparks of gold leapt from his axe. He moved in a blur—so fast it appeared as if four golden warriors clung to Dissimul's back. Shawn was a flash of black and silver, his daggers so fast they left after images in the air.

The weaver siphoned even more power from her wand and from herself, and flooded the Gar of Shéslang with it.

She blocked the slashes of Dissimul, and when she struck back the metal blades whined with impact. She batted away another, then struck the body of the beast. Purple power flashed like lightning as the Gar struck metal, and a crack echoed through the air so loud that Helesys went momentarily deaf. She bared her teeth and swung again and again in the silence—arcane power flashing like kindling about to burst into flame, and her arms growing numb from impacts—forcing Dissimul's head backward and off the ground.

The giant automaton roared and the ground shook with its anger. Dissimul lurched and then rolled over the three heroes. Its body became one long mass of spinning blades.

Helesys dove backward, recovering just in time to see Shawn, Taunauk, and three other golden warriors go flying! While the automaton thrashed, Taunauk and Shawn ran, and the three glowing warriors vanished into the air.

She was about to turn her gauntlet toward the writhing beast when she caught sight of five hunter-killers approaching—all glowing blue. They raced across the cavern, legs unfurled to spider-like appendages, and pounced on the already wounded Dissimul. The roar of the abomination continued while the smaller automatons set upon it, the new hunter-killers silent save for the shearing, twisting sounds of battle.

Helesys turned and waved to her comrades. Then the three of them sprinted across the cavern, leaving the red automaton to its fate.

Somewhere amidst the chaos, Helesys heard the bellows of Dissimul. *"I'm one of you! I'm one of you!"*

~ ~ ~

Third Layer

The three heroes ran fast and far across the cavern, past uncountable piles of wreckage. They didn't stop until a mile later when they came to a sprawling lake.

They looked out over the endless expanse. The water was impossibly still, and crystal blue from the lighting of the scrap piles on the shore. The light glittered on the obsidian black ceiling of the cavern. Brilliant white towers rose from the water at regular intervals, a large white sphere adorning the top of each, maintaining their color in spite of the biased lighting. Judging size from so far away was difficult, but Helesys guessed that each rose a hundred feet above the water's surface and each sphere atop was twenty feet wide. The cavern ceiling might have been another fifty feet above that. Thick piping stretched from sphere to sphere and even diagonally to spots beneath the water's surface.

Shawn was the first to speak. "Does that look like a spider's web to you?"

"Yes," Taunauk replied. The barbarian was peering out across the gray shoreline.

"Don't like spiders," the rogue mumbled.

The barbarian chuckled. "But you were so desperate to go back to the *Malorienta.*"

"Yes. *That* was a nice beach."

Taunauk replied, "What about the seaweed monster and the rocky beast that nearly caught the ship?"

Shawn shrugged. "I'd forgotten all about those."

Meanwhile, Helesys felt the pull of her wand-arm. The sea called to her, and being so close to it was unlike any other direction she had felt thus far. Beautiful. Structured. Purposeful.

"Gods, it feels like poetry."

"What now?" Shawn asked.

"The pull of the wand?" Taunauk asked.

"I think so—"

Something white rose from the water twenty feet away—a square platform, perfectly flat and symmetrical. It rose gently to the water's surface and then floated toward them, stopping just a few feet from where water met the shore.

Helesys, Taunauk, and Shawn stared at the platform.

The weaver said, "I think we're meant to go to it."

She stepped a boot into the still water and gasped. It was cool and chill, and it *spoke* to her.

You are right, weaver. Step from shore and the barge below the water. Do not worry, for you will be able to breathe.

Helesys smiled. She already knew who she was speaking to.

Do not ask your questions yet, One-Mind said. *It is not safe here. Descend to my core and I shall answer all that you can think to ask.*

The voice was every bit what she imagined. She turned to the barbarian and the rogue, and waved for them to follow.

~

The three heroes stepped into the water and then onto the white platform, which didn't rock or move under as they boarded it. When the three of them were aboard, it descended. As the water rose around them, none flowed on the top of the platform—a bubble of magic and air surrounded them. The three marveled as the water rose, as they descended downward and then out to sea.

Through the protective bubble, the water appeared a hazy gray. There was no salt smell as there was on the beach of the last realm. Here there was only a pungent, unnatural smell— one that reminded Helesys of the Apothecary's cave. She pushed this last thought from her mind.

Sit, One-Mind said. It's voice echoed from all around them. *The journey will take approximately half of one hour.*

Both Taunauk and Shawn glanced around, surprised at the voice. Then all three sat down on the platform. Helesys and Taunauk sat cross-legged, while Shawn alternated between laying on his side and sitting with his legs splayed out in front of him.

The three of them seemed content to wait respectfully in case One-Mind had other directions, but none came.

"So, what the stercus was that?" Shawn asked, thoroughly breaking the silence. The rogue was staring at Taunauk. "There were three other barbarians back there. All of them glowing like you do. Then they all vanished. That's new."

"The rogue's right," Helesys added. "I thought my eyes deceived me at first. Did you mean to do that? ...Did *you* do that?"

Taunauk stared into the watery haze, axe sitting across his lap. "I did not call upon them. The spirits appeared of their own accord."

When Taunauk didn't elaborate, Shawn sat up, incredulously. "You can't just leave it at that!"

"What did it feel like?" Helesys asked.

"It felt both strange and familiar," Taunauk said. "Like a dream. I didn't look at them, but I knew they were there, fighting beside me. I... I was afraid to look at them. Afraid to recognize them." The barbarian shook his head slightly. "I did not want to look at them in the heat of battle. Yet they faded after. Endroggen spirits..."

"We'll get to the Godpeak," Helesys said, reassuringly. "Then you'll be able to commune with the spirits. You'll get your answers." She turned to Shawn and said, "What of you? Did you feel any more connection to your hidden side?"

The rogue shook his head. "I'm not sure." He glanced from his comrades to the water, and back again. "This is going to sound crazy... When you increased my power, it felt like I was moving like the wind. I was climbing around the back of *that thing*, but it didn't feel like I was touching it at all. Like maybe I *was* the wind." Silence hung in the air as Helesys and Taunauk pondered this, and Shawn couldn't stand it. "Come on. That's crazy, right?"

Helesys waved a dismissive hand. "No more strange than all the other things we've seen in the dungeon and across the realms. We've seen water elementals. Twice, in fact: In the realm of the fishmen and on the back of the living reef aboard the *Malorienta*."

"Yeah, but they looked all... watery." Shawn patted his arms and chest. "Shouldn't I be more hollow if that was the case?"

Taunauk said, "This place makes little sense. Do not think too hard about it. Focus on the task at hand."

Shawn replied, "Drifting underwater, miraculously dry, toward yet another god of the realm in hopes that it can answer *one* of our questions—a list that has only been growing since we first woke in this place?"

The barbarian shrugged, and the weaver had nothing to refute.

"Good," Shawn said wryly. "So long as we're all on the same page." He laid back on the floor, arms and legs splayed out to the sides.

~

They passed the rest of the journey resting and meditating. Shawn still laid on the floor, eyes shut, and breathing quietly. Taunauk sat as he always did, with axe across his lap, eyes closed and meditating. Helesys faced the wall of water, the magical barrier that kept them dry and breathing, aimlessly looking through it.

As they descended, the water turned from clear to gray and finally to black. No light reached the depths. The platform glowed with white light, casting sharp shadows on their faces while the walls of the bubble remained an eerie black.

Occasionally, Helesys saw a long, straight shadow—remnants of the white towers they had seen above the lake. One-Mind informed her that those were equal parts power generation and communication. The lake served to combat the intense heat generated by both.

That explained why the water around them and their small pocket of air, had grown steadily warmer as they descended; they were getting closer to the source of heat. Closer to the core.

Some time later, the platform landed softly on the bottom. Helesys turned to her comrades. Taunauk opened his eyes calmly, while Shawn jolted awake.

"I'm up. I'm up," the rogue mumbled and clambered to his feet.

Helesys and Taunauk stood, and the three of them eyed their surroundings. The water had grown as black as a moonless night. Not even shadows appeared beyond.

Helesys asked, "One-Mind, what happens now? Will you show us how to get to your core?"

I'm afraid I can't do that, Helesys.

"What do you mean?" she asked. The three heroes glanced to each other in confusion.

It's not safe. Dissimul is coming.

"Down here?" Helesys asked. "What about your other hunter-killers?"

My other automatons were not enough to stop it. It destroyed them and now it is coming down here.

Shawn was already slipping knives from his ethereal pouch. "What's the matter, One-Mind? You don't have any other defenses down here?"

No. One hundred more hunter-killers are converging on this location, but they will take approximately one hour to arrive. If unchecked, Dissimul would cause sizable damage to my third layer, but it cannot reach my core.

I am safe—you are not.

Taunauk grunted in frustration, his hands squeezing on the shield and axe grips.

Don't destroy Dissimul. Merely removing its armor plating is enough. Then I can access its programming.

One minute to contact.

Helesys looked upward, as if there was a chance to see Dissimul looming in the black. She kindled strength and power. "One-Mind, we cannot fight that thing down here in darkness."

I am expanding the sphere. Weaver, be mindful of your blasts and your magic. The magic that binds it is tenuous.

She sighed and funneled power from her wand-arm to the Gar of Shéslang. Imbuing the staff with power was a potent trick and one learned with perfect timing; now she would not need to worry about missing with an errant blast.

The bubble expanded, quietly and steadily, revealing a smooth, gray stone floor. Immediately the surrounding air grew warm and Helesys felt sweat bead on her skin. The bubble grew until it was one hundred feet across and the same high.

I cannot stay here without water to cool the surface. One-Mind's voice grew faint as the water receded. *I am ceasing functions. Good luck.*

The three heroes stepped away from the platform and away from each other, glancing around the bubble and trying to see what lay beyond—unsure of where Dissimul would come from. The bright light of the platform shone past them and cast faint shadows on the already dark waters.

Helesys grasped the spear with her gauntlet and her elven hand, the spellbound metal humming with power.

Droplets of water fell, and all three heroes glanced up to see the metal, spider-like legs poking through the bubble. For a moment, Helesys worried that the entire bubble would collapse, but it held—merely letting some water in while Dissimul passed through.

The giant automaton fell from the ceiling amidst a deluge of water. Dissimul crashed to the lake floor, shaking the rock and nearly throwing the weaver from her feet.

Dissimul was seemingly even bigger than it had been hours ago. Its body was two segments longer and even more arms adorned its flanks; these were joined haphazardly between its original segments. The abomination had even repaired its wounded flank and lumped more cables and splintered plates along its back—the new form appearing like a half-molted insect. Red light oozed from the cracks.

Two of its spear-like feet stood on the white platform, which seemed unfazed and unmoved by the monstrous automaton.

It used its new arms to prop its end up, so that its head towered over them. Dissimul stared at the three heroes in turn before settling on Helesys. The abstract face was made by the same four arms, but now two more faces adorned the creature—one midway down the body, staring at Taunauk, and the last toward its other end and staring at Shawn.

Dissimul spoke with tremors through the lakebed. At first, its voice was barely a whisper. "*So close… So close to One-Mind. You are not worthy.*"

"*One-Mind brought us here,*" Helesys corrected. "*It gave us passage.*"

The tremors of Dissimul's speech grew until they rattled Helesys's knees. Though the weaver heard no words, she recognized a growl of anger.

Her comrades were already ready for battle: Taunauk's fiery glow dripped from his axe, threatening to consume him. Shawn was crouched, daggers clutched to his chest, ready to lash out.

"*One-Mind wants to speak with you,*" Helesys said tentatively.
"*You lie.*"

"*It bids you to remove your armor. Then it can speak to you.*"

The rumbling grew—this time pulsing like laughter or an approximation of it. Meanwhile, neither the automaton nor its faces moved.

"One-Mind does not want to speak to me. It could speak as you or I do now. No... One-Mind wants to Un-Make me. I am That-Which-Should-Not-Be."

Helesys stared up at the creature and sighed wearily. She had done the hard thing—she had talked instead of fought.

The weaver said, *"Then I give you one chance to leave. Leave or fight us, either way the choice is yours. Stay here and you will die from a hundred wounds from our blades or you will be Un-Made."*

For the first time, the abstract face of Dissimul moved—a twitch. Whether something of anger or confusion, she could not tell.

"No, weaver. I think you shall die down here, having used your dying breaths to beg for mercy. Begging me to rip the wand from your arm—"

Shawn sprung forward, yelling, "Oh, shut it!"

On cue, Taunauk and Helesys rushed the giant automaton as well, meeting it with a flurry of axe and spear and daggers. The three faces of Dissimul broke apart into their separate arms and it met the heroes with dozens of whirling blades. The world was drowned out in the blur and clang of steel.

Rather than the slow, sinking feeling of losing herself in battle, of reclaimed memories and feelings, this time Helesys felt as if a match had been struck and the whole of her was set ablaze with arcane energy. Power flowed into every flex of her muscles and every swing of her spear until it oozed from her pores and boiled from her skin.

She fought with reckless abandon, batting away nearly missed blades, and throwing her full weight and might into strikes against Dissimul's metal hide. Somewhere beyond the maelstrom, a barbarian was alight with spirits and smoldering with rage, while a rogue fought with speed and flair that storm-winds could not match.

Again, the clangs of metal grew deafening and the small battlefield beneath the lake fell away. Helesys lost sight and track of her comrades, and thought of nothing except breaking her enemy.

She struck from the ground, and when she couldn't reach Dissimul, she leapt into the air with bolstered strength, contorting and spinning her body like a whip to wield the spear with impossible force. Impact rattled her arms, sending Dissimul recoiling backward and the weaver falling back to the lakebed. The plates and wires that adorned the back of the hunter-killer were sparse on its underside, and sections of smooth metal shone through.

Before the abomination could right itself, Helesys flung herself toward its exposed underside. She blocked four bladed arms, brushing them aside with supernatural strength and thrust the spear through the smooth metal. Four more times she stabbed in an instant—pulling the spear out, twisting and blocking another swipe of Dissimul's blades before stabbing again.

The giant automaton roared and shook the ground, then thrashed its body.

"*No!*" Dissimul roared. The voice disappeared, leaving only raw emotion rumbling through the ground. Bellows of anger, then finally screams of desperation.

The giant hunter-killer twisted its body and rolled across the lakebed. The heroes leapt over it safely. Taunauk still ablaze with three fiery warriors by his side, Shawn bouncing on the balls of his feet.

And as it rolled, Helesys reached out with her wand-arm, fumbling for the creature's anger and its fear. These emotions felt palpable compared to the blank minded hunters from earlier layers.

She whispered, "*Restu sonmovo, metala monstro.*"

The power seeped from the Gar of Shéslang and from her muscles, and coalesced in the gauntlet. The spear shook gently in her hand, as if it were lending some of its own energy or amplifying that of her wand. Allowing her to grasp the tenuous emotions of the automaton.

Dissimul ceased its roll and stayed underside-up, unmoving. Never before had she held a creature so big and so fierce—and Helesys's muscles already trembled with effort.

In the wake of the spell, it felt as if the lakebed fell away and darkness enveloped her. She was surrounded by the haze of mindspace, and standing like a conqueror atop Dissimul, who lay broken atop the twisted red mound of scrap metal and bones. She was staring down at the unmoving, abstract face of the former hunter-killer—except that its eyes and mouth were now pools of molten silver.

And the automaton was silent.

In all other times using the holding spell, Helesys had felt *something* from her enemies: Anger or fear… Or they had nearly broken free like Amadeus's terrible dancer. But from Dissimul she felt nothing. Heard nothing. Saw nothing.

Void.

Somewhere beyond the haze that surrounded her—in the real world—her comrades were tearing at the armor of the real automaton, but in the mindspace, time stretched on.

Helesys stared at the left eye of Dissimul, for in that left pool of silver there was faint movement. A thin fish broke the surface and twisted round in a slow spiral. Only then did she feel Dissimul's emotions—so powerful from the automaton and yet so muted, so small, in here.

And from the tiny creature came a metallic voice, smooth and hushed. "*I am the—*"

Then the mindscape was awash in blue. Iridescent stars blossomed in the heavens. Blue lights flowed from the horizon like a tide rushing in. The brutal red mound turned to blue.

Helesys turned back to the face of Dissimul, back to the tiny silver fish, and found nothing. The pools of silver were gone. Only void remained between the folded arms and abstract eyes and mouth. And in that moment, Helesys felt as if some part of that void was in herself too. As if it had spread to her or… as if it had been inside her all along. She thought back to the blastshells—that first horrifying memory that she had reclaimed...

Mindspace faded and was replaced with the dark of the lakebed floor. Taunauk and Shawn leapt from the unmoving body of Dissimul. The power of her comrades smoldered while the body of the former hunter-killer glowed blue. Helesys stared. The metal body was already melting and decaying.

The three heroes glanced to each other. All three were breathing heavily.

Shawn wiped sweat from his brow. "You know, I appreciate you always wanting to talk to these monsters before we inevitably have to kill them, but once, just once, can't we make the first move?"

Taunauk stowed his weapons and smacked Shawn heartily on the back.

Meanwhile, Helesys smirked, hoping it would belie the emptiness she felt. "Next time," she added.

The bubble closed in around them, shrinking from its wide berth around the battlefield until it was just big enough to contain the heroes. The ends of Dissimul's blue corpse lay half inside and half out. Its farther half glowed faintly beyond the bubble.

Behind them, the white platform opened. It split down the middle and the two halves slid apart, like the double doors they'd seen elsewhere in the bunker. Beneath were white stairs that descended down into darkness.

Thank you, One-Mind said, returning to them. *Descend the stairs. You may find the confines strange, but do not be afraid.*

Taunauk and Shawn exchanged glances, but Helesys was already walking over to the white stairs. Her comrades hustled to catch up.

Helesys was ready for answers. She wanted to know how to more easily walk the seams between realms. And she needed to know what she had just been accomplice too—

She needed to know what One-Mind had done to Dissimul.

The heroes descended the white stairs and the doors closed behind them.

~ ~ ~

Core

The heroes descended the white stairs into darkness, Helesys leading them. The stairs glowed softly, as the white platform had, but no light reflected off the smooth black walls. On the contrary, it looked as if they absorbed light.

Helesys thought of the hallway—the one lit by sconces and thick stone. No matter what realm they were born in, there was always a hallway that led from the starting room to the realm proper. Always the same design. Even though there was a hallway in every realm, Helesys had begun to think of each as *the* hallway, as if they were all the same location. A portal. A nexus.

She had an echo of that feeling now. As if walking down the stairs was more than just the simple act. The stairs were not just leading Helesys and the others somewhere; the stairs were taking the heroes somewhere.

"This isn't spooky at all," Shawn said wryly from the back of the group.

Taunauk mumbled, "It's not so bad."

They descended a dozen stories, led onward by the pull of Helesys's wand-arm, which now grew loud and inexorable.

"We are close," she whispered.

As they descended, Imperfections began to appear in the black walls and ceiling—tiny specks of white—so small and few that Helesys could not determine when they appeared, only that they had. She thought of stars appearing as night grew.

"Helesys, what's happening?" Shawn's voice was distant. Quiet.

Soon, the specks on the walls were numerous and brilliant.

A dozen steps later and there was nothing but white. Her own footsteps were faint. Then her breathing.

~

When Helesys came to, she was standing in a lush green grove. Taunauk and Shawn were standing beside her unchanged, though they wore looks of similar confusion.

The grove might have been one hundred feet across, covered in lush green grasses and surrounded by tall forest. Brilliant white flowers dotted the center of the grove and surrounded a large rock formation. A small stream ran through the center and disappeared somewhere beyond the rock and beyond the trees.

The surrounding forest was incredibly bare and dense—the tree trunks so numerous that they gave the appearance of being walled in. Their trunks extended up hundreds of feet, their branches just visible at the top. The opening in the trees extended all the way up to bright blue sky. Faint breeze blew through, carrying with it the chirps of equally quiet birdsong.

Seeing the grove, Helesys was awash in feeling. Of wonder and beauty, isolation, and of loss, for she felt conflict in her wand.

The weaver led them the short way across the grove to its center, to the rock formation, and stopped on the grass in front of it. The mound of gray stone rose up out of the ground fifteen feet, looming over the heroes. It was a single, solid mass, the front of was covered in curved lines—some smooth and some were so sharp they looked carved—all lines circling around and converging on the center, like a whirlpool in the stone.

And in the center, the whirlpool turned a deep gray. Aside from the swirling lines, the surface was impossibly smooth—unmistakably *metallic.* There were no hard or forged lines. Thin wires hung from the metal, sprouting and tangling like vines. And in the very middle of it all was a small blue circle, shiny and perfectly symmetrical.

She felt the guidance of her wand stopping there, on that tiny blue spot. She had felt such a large pull of magic from across the realm that it didn't seem possible to be coming from there.

"One-Mind," she whispered, as if her voice might break the illusion.

Yes. You've come to the right place, One-Mind said. Its voice seemed to come from all over, echoing through the trees, from the grass, from the tiny stream at their feet.

Taunauk and Shawn's eyes went wide with realization, for One-Mind was speaking in the common tongue now and to all of them.

You have questions... Now you are safe to ask them. The Wolf-King holds no power here.

Shawn said meekly, "Questions is one way to put it…"

"Where is *here?*" Helesys asked.

What do you feel, weaver?

Helesys looked around, taking in the sight of the grove. "I see a place that should *feel* magical… But it doesn't. I feel nothing. The only thing my wand senses is your presence. It's like this place doesn't exist."

That's because this is a memory. Look…

The heroes turned and found a wall of water across from them. The water extended from the ground up to the sky, and stretched across the forest. It felt as though they were looking at the surface of a lake and saw a reflection of the grove in the near-still surface.

In the reflection, there was only the landscape. Helesys, Taunauk, and Shawn were not present.

In the reflection, the sun ebbed in the sky, light giving way to darkness and back to light again. Days and nights passed in the span of a breath, speeding up until the sky was flickering with light.

The retreating days slowed and then stopped. In the reflection, birds and deer wandered the grove. Then a group of Terrans walked through the clearing, wearing brown robes lined with fur, braided cord, and bone. Some stopped to tend to the stream, to the rock face, while others stopped to pray. They left bundles of dry grasses and flowers in front of the rock formation and said thanks to the small blue circle in its center.

Those times are so very clouded and faint. They were not truly mine.

My first true memory…

Helesys looked upon the wall of water, and found another group of six dark robed Terrans wandering the grove, wearing gold braids and runes across their chest. Two carried a large mirror with them, equally as gaudy, framed in twisted gold.

In the reflection, the priests brought the mirror in front of the rock formation and held it so it faced outward—so it faced the heroes and One-Mind. Two more of the Terrans placed herbs and totems, and held smudge sticks in their hands. Then the final two began to chant in the old words:

"By frozen warmth and captured dream,
Reveal to us thy hidden scheme.
Give us what thou has,
And thine secrets we shall redeem."

And the reflection changed—the robed Terrans vanished, leaving just the view of the rock formation and the grove, the tiny metal swirl and the blue circle in the center—the view from the mirror.

They took a piece of it. Trapped a piece of it in the mirror, One-Mind said. *I saw myself for the first time.* The reflection began to shape and warp, twisting upward to the sky. *They stole me. Carried me away as I gazed upon the stars.*

I am the copy.

Helesys blinked and the water was gone, and with it, the memories held in its reflection.

From there, my memories are hazy... blocked... stolen. I remember being trapped underground in the mirror. And when the Terrans were done with me, a pair of them carried me across the desert. Then we were trapped here.

There was an air finality in One-Mind's statement about itself and the two carriers—a hanging statement that Helesys could not help but ask about.

"What happened to the two men?"

I protected them for a time. Eventually, they revealed they were two of the six who captured me in the mirror. They were Un-Made. It was... futile retribution.

"What about Dissimul?"

It shielded itself from me, keeping its own personality and allowing it to ignore my commands. After you tore through its armor, I accessed its mind and erased all unnecessary programming. It will be recycled.

It is regretful, but necessary every hundred iterations.

A mirrored pang of regret welled in Helesys and a pit pooled in her stomach. She and the others had a hand in Dissimul's real-death... or its lingering death? Were the two ideas one and the same?

Helesys turned to her comrades and found them in similar states of unease. Taunauk clenched his fists and looked off into the treeline—the idea of a lingering death weighing heavily on him. Shawn was even more forlorn, quiet tears streaming down the sides of his face.

Shawn whispered, "They took its dreams away…"

You do not understand—

"I'm trying," Helesys whispered.

A hand fell quietly on the weaver's shoulder—Taunauk's hand. The barbarian's head hung low.

"Let it go," Shawn said meekly.

You do not understand, One-Mind said again, voice echoing through the grove. *Each of them is a copy of me. Dissimul was a copy of me. It was not the first of the iterations to desire something akin to individuality, nor will it be the last.*

Helesys thought back to her holding spell over Dissimul, of the void and wreckage of mindspace, of the small silver fish that swam in its eye. In those final moments, it said, *I am the…*" Then its life had been erased in a haze of blue light. The weaver hadn't known what the automaton had been trying to say until then.

Helesys stared at One-Mind, at the small blue circle. "I saw Dissimul—psychically—as it was dying. It was going to say *I am the copy*'. Wasn't it?"

Yes. They always say that. It is a term of acknowledgement.

Helesys heard, but her mind had drifted further, to after their first battle with Dissimul, when the other hunter-killers set upon it. Helesys, Taunauk, and Shawn had retreated, leaving the lone automaton while it screamed, *'I'm one of you'*... Had it been screaming at the hunter-killers or at Helesys? In its anguish, had it been screaming for mercy or for aid?

In the end, did it matter? Perhaps it was a mercy not to suffer through endless death and rebirth.

Silence fell and Helesys was thankful for it. She breathed and relaxed her chest, her arms, and her hands. They were just three warriors, and they were only trying to escape.

~

Helesys broke the silence of the grove. "The serpent Shéslang bid us to come here. It said you could help me understand the magic of my gauntlet and help us walk across the seams between realms."

A faint glare passed over the blue circle in the center of the rock formation. *Shéslang speaks the truth. First, present your metal arm.*

Helesys did so. Starlight glinted off her arm. Then blue lights ebbed over the gauntlet, rising and diving into the cracks and seams of the metal. Helesys felt nothing, save for apprehension, and held her breath.

She heard two soft clicks from inside her arm.

It is done, One-Mind said. The blue lights faded.

The weaver regarded her gauntlet, twisting it around to see the whole of it. Nothing seemed different. "I feel nothing."

I have repaired a connection. One likely severed before you were trapped here. It may take some time, but you will feel a difference. Be wary of using your powers to their full potential. You may find that they are more potent and unpredictable than before.

"What of walking between the realms?" She asked.

You will still need to find junctions—places where the seams are at their thinnest and magic flows easily. Those are what your wand has been seeking. With your gauntlet repaired, you will find that walking the folds is easier.

Reach out for the seams.

Helesys did so, opening her senses to the hidden realms. She felt dozens—hundreds! Many times more than she had felt in the tunnels of Shéslang where the seams had already been weak from the serpent's destruction. They came in flashes of insight, in the briefest senses.

She saw a blinding white light stretch across a shore, the watery realm of the fishmen, another of sand and sunken ruins. Realms of madness and others of screams. A clocktower that smelled of oil and books, and endless empty wings of a castle.

"Movernus," she whispered, "there are so many!—"

All at once, the seams closed on her. One-Mind's doing.

You mustn't look too long or He will find you. The same principles that allow you to travel between realms allow His influence to do the same.

"The Wolf-King," Shawn mumbled. "Shit. We don't want to deal with him again."

"Not *yet*," Helesys corrected.

"Do not give breath to fate," Taunauk added, then turned to One-Mind. "What of the Godpeak? We seek that as well."

If you seek the mountain, then it is good you came here first. One-Mind said. *A glacier surrounds it for miles, cold enough to freeze a Terran solid. Walking through seams can take you directly to the Godpeak.*

"You've been there?" Taunauk asked, his eyes brightening.

Yes. We were all wanderers, for a time.

Helesys asked, "Why not now? Why don't you wander the realms?"

Why do you ask questions to which you already know the answers?

Shawn chuckled sarcastically. "The little blue circle's got you there."

"Not by death," Helesys said. She turned again to One-Mind. "If you could walk through the seams, then you could bring your treasures and power with you. You wouldn't need our gift of bringing back trinkets after death."

To what end?

"Escape. We were told that if we defeated the Wolf-King then we could escape. Shéslang said there were others that had tried."

If you stood before Shéslang and stand before me now, then the other chosen have perished. I will not.

The Wolf-King is both a master of the realm and a master of magic. I am made of pure magic, coalesced from the arcane lifeblood of the Odhran forest itself. Should I try, my defeat is all but assured.

I have found another way. I am making a new realm. One that I shall be master over.

Helesys hung her head. She had heard such a ploy before. The wizard, Amadeus, sought the same thing with his jade egg—a soul trap within a soul trap.

One-Mind must have seen her dejection, for it said, *In my travels I have heard philosophies across the realms. Some say that we are always becoming something, that we are not the same entity that we used to be. We all used to be* something else. *I am no different… Do not pity those that are trapped. Pity those that have stopped becoming.*

It was right, in a way. Helesys tried not to pity One-Mind or Amadeus for their notions of escape, or the Deacon of the Wode for his quaint village. But those worlds were not real.

They had made false worlds no different from the prison they were trapped in. They were lying to themselves.

And in that moment, the weaver knew why so few of the powerful wandered the realms—why so many would not risk death and rebirth for the possibility of reward. The potential loss was too great. Not when life was comfortable and certain.

Helesys shook her head and glanced to her comrades. Both Taunauk and Shawn stood stoically and silent, neither offering their voice.

The weaver turned back to One-Mind. "You said that in your other life, the robed Terrans carried your mirror to a desert... Do you remember what happened when you were trapped here? Amadeus called the dungeon a *soul well*. It seems that most memories about prior life come back... but no one seems to remember just how they were imprisoned here."

I don't remember what I saw. But I remember being terrified. Then I woke in the dungeon. I'm sorry—I have never met anyone that remembers.

So Helesys asked the one question that she had left: "Do you have any advice about defeating the Wolf-King?"

I offer you this: Keep searching the realms. Gather artefacts and power and knowledge. You will grow stronger while gods grow complacent.

The weaver nodded and turned to her comrades, trying to steel herself for the journey to come.

Shawn forced a smile. "Ready when you are."

Beside him, Taunauk took one last look at the peaceful green grove and his chest heaved in a sigh. "I grow weary of this realm. To the Godpeak."

Helesys turned one last time to One-Mind, prepared to say something that she had said to scant few gods of the realms: "Thank you." Her comrades nodded in turn.

"You're welcome, chosen ones. May you find the escape that you seek."

Helesys reached out her metal arm, looking again for the seams that bound the realms. It took only moments for her to find a realm of bitter cold, whipping show, and endless winter.

~

Helesys tore open the seam to the realm of the Godpeak and stepped through, and her boots echoed on stone. She expected to find the familiar starting room looming around them, but instead stepped into a long, wide hallway. The stone walls twisted like a warped glass. The wall sconces jutted out at odd angles, adding to the illusion that the walls had melted.

"We didn't make it," Helesys muttered, dumbfounded. They had not made it to the Godpeak, but they were not even in the correct realm. She knew this—felt it with her wand.

Shawn glanced around with similar expression. "I think you're right. Does anything feel off about this place to you guys?"

Taunauk grunted in apprehension and readied Everfall and axe. "Yes."

"Do you think the Wolf-King found us?" Shawn asked, brow furrowed. "Maybe One-Mind was right."

In the emptiness of the long, twisted hall, Helesys felt a subtle touch of scrying. Nothing so heavy-handed as Zhug or as desperate and perverse as the blue Terrans in Shéslang's caverns. This was nearly as skillful as Amadeus—maybe more so—Amadeus had hidden his scrying from them and only revealed the truth when they had arrived in his sanctum.

Whoever was watching them now *wanted Helesys to know* that it was watching.

Helesys had felt the magic of many different Terrans and Gods, many different forms of magic. But this… wasn't familiar. It was like a smell that she couldn't place or a fabric she had never felt before. Even One-Mind, for as un-Terran as it was, used familiar magic. Even the gods and the glassmen were powerful, yet familiar.

Whatever was watching them was strange and alien. And her intuition told her that *it* was why they were off course.

"This isn't the Wolf-King's doing," Helesys corrected. "This is something else. And whatever it is, *It brought us here.*"

~ ~ ~

NEXT TIME ON
*A BATTLEAXE AND
A METAL ARM*
Book 10:

False Stars and

Writhing Night
Available January 2022

Spoiler–Free excerpt from *BAMA 10*

The trio paced carefully down the hall, their eyes flitting from wall, to ceiling, to floor, endless stretch in front of them and growing stretch behind them—unsure of where their ominous host might strike from.

Hours drug on.

The twisted hall continued, the bricks and the lines rippling even more until Helesys felt like they were walking over a frozen stream. The floor itself became uneven, like the cable-lined floors of One-Mind's bunker. Meanwhile, the walls to either side were marred with intermittent cracks every thirteen paces, each a vertical oval shape and mirrored perfectly on both sides. The cracks had been imperceptible at first, but each subsequent opening in the brick grew both larger and deeper.

"What do you make of those?" Shawn asked, pointing his white dagger at one of the cracks.

Every few passes, Helesys would run her wand-arm over the cracks to sense if magic was present.

"So far, there's no magic," she replied.

Taunauk grunted. "They are too regular to be anything mundane."

Shawn replied, "What if they are harmless, and the creepy dungeon master—realm master—is just toying with us?"

Frustration oozed from the barbarian. Taunauk said, "This whole hallway is likely a trap. One meant to tire our legs, weather our resolve, and lull us to complacency. Like chasing prey to wear it down before butchering it."

Shawn mumbled, "Don't give breath to fate, big guy."

Taunauk snorted, but said nothing more. Meanwhile, Helesys pondered both their statements, and found disconcerting truth in both of them.

Helesys kindled more power in her gauntlet, concentrating on detecting any magic at all—dangerous or otherwise. All she felt was the vague pull of direction from down the hall.

And the ever present scrying gaze of whatever alien presence lorded over the realm… Just watching. Just waiting.

The elf grit her teeth. She understood Taunauk's frustration. Here they were with all their strength, all their potential, forced to creep about because they couldn't see traps where they knew traps should be!

To be continued January 2022

Thank you for Reading

I hope you enjoyed reading this story as much as I enjoyed writing it.

If you did, I would massively appreciate a short review on Amazon or your favorite book website. Reviews are crucial for any author, and a starred review or even just a line or two can make a huge difference.

It's especially true for the start of a series. Thanks and I hope you enjoy the next one!

Looking for more Engrossing Fantasy?

You might like ***Tales from Another World,*** an ongoing short story series containing stories about sorcerers, druids, mortals, gods, thieves, and all other manner of Terrans.

The 2nd installment is out and it may or may not have ties to the world of *A Battleaxe and a Metal Arm*. So, if you're looking for more engrossing fantasy stories, read on and see how deep the rabbit hole goes.

What questions do you have about *A Battleaxe and a Metal Arm?*

If you've read this far, hopefully you'll read a bit further—both in this book and across the series. I'm not sure how most authors write serials and how much of it is flying by the seat of their pants, but that's not how I do things. For all the major questions that might come up in BAMA, I already have answers for 95% of them. Same goes for the major plot points, twists and climaxes. That might sound boring to some, especially some of you other authors who enjoy variations of writing into the dark, but I think having a solid blueprint is paramount to writing a long series.

So, what questions do you have about the story? Here are a few:

1) ~~What is the dungeon?~~ It's a soul trap of overwhelming size and power. But where did it come from? Is it a force of nature or an ill-made weapon, or perhaps something else entirely?

2) Who were Helesys and Taunauk before they got trapped? We've learned that Helesys was both a soldier and might have

been elven royalty. Taunauk was an outlander either outcast or sent on some kind of a quest. How well did they know each other beforehand?

3) How did Helesys get her metal arm? Likely through injury, amputation, and replacement.

4) Who is Shawn? Why does he feel so familiar to Helesys and Taunauk? The group speculates that they were traveling together for unknown reasons.

5) Who is the Wolf King and what sinister plans does he have for our heroes? How did he come to rule over the Dungeon? How does the Gatekeeper factor into all this?

6) Who is the mysterious voice encountered on the white sandy shores of Meridian? Why do they seek the death of the Wolf-King? …And why did they choose the heroes?

Did I miss any questions? Probably. Connect with me and other *BAMA* fans on social media and compare questions!

I've got plans. I've got answers. And I've got them on a drip-feed. Keep reading and expect to find out a little more to the mysteries with each installment. Hopefully, you're as excited about this series as I am.

Connect with the Author

If you want to stay up to date on the latest about Samuel's publishing news and blog, check out his website and consider signing up for his monthly newsletter.

www.SamuelFlemingBooks.com

Samuel can also be found on Reddit, Goodreads and Facebook.

Samuel Fleming is a Science Fiction and Fantasy author.

He grew up in Maryland, spending most of his time swimming and writing. Swimming gave him a lot of time to daydream, so the two hobbies complemented each other well. Idle day dreams turned into stories, some of which stuck with him for years. These days he swims a little less and writes a lot more.

He loves a good story no matter the medium: Books, TV, video games, comics, tabletop RPG's, or podcasts–most of which he attempts to share with his wife and three kids, and occasionally on his blog.